WHAT'S THE MATTER, HABIBI?

WRITTEN AND ILLUSTRATED BY BETSY LEWIN

CLARION BOOKS/NEW YORK

To the Cairo NESA delegates
who helped develop this story.

Special thanks to Judith Heide Gilliland
for naming the camel.

Clarion Books • a Houghton Mifflin Company imprint • 215 Park Avenue South, New York,
NY 10003 • Copyright © 1997 by Betsy Lewin • The illustrations were executed in watercolor.
• The text was set in 16-point Horley. • All rights reserved. • For information about permission
to reproduce selections from this book, write to Permissions, Houghton Mifflin Company,
215 Park Avenue South, New York, NY 10003.

www.houghtonmifflinbooks.com

Printed in China

Library of Congress Cataloging-in-Publication Data

What's the matter, Habibi? / written and illustrated by Betsy Lewin.
            p.   cm.
Summary: One day, instead of following Ahmed around in a circle giving
children rides, Habibi the camel runs through the bazaar with Ahmed
following him and trying to figure out what is wrong.
ISBN 0-395-85816-X   PA ISBN 0-618-43242-6
[1. Camels—Fiction. 2. Egypt—Fiction.] I. Title.
PZ7.L58417Wh 1997
[E]—dc21   96-52440
CIP
AC

SCP 10 9 8 7 6 5 4 3

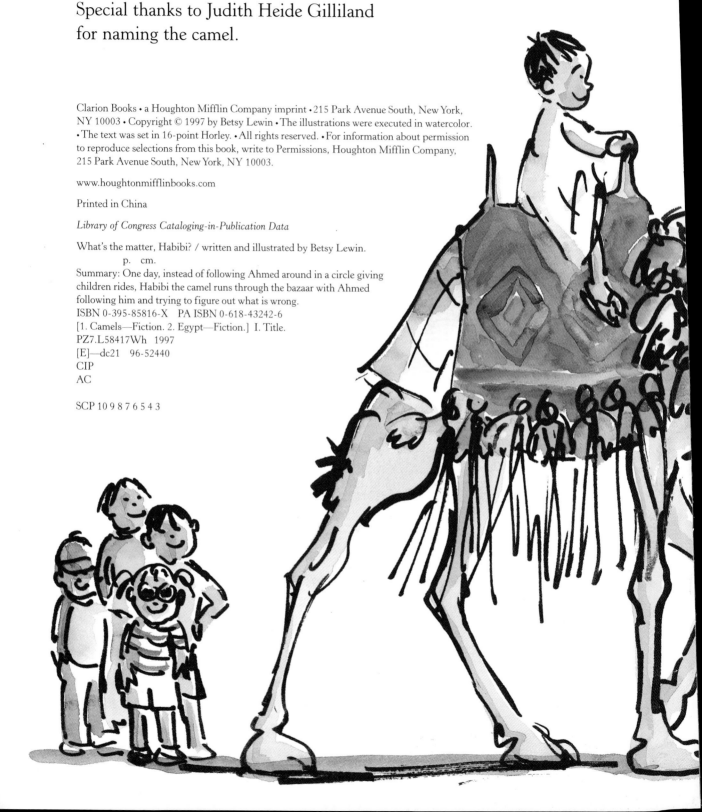

Every day Habibi followed Ahmed around in a circle giving rides to children. Habibi's big, round feet went ploppity-plop, ploppity-plop in the sand.

But one day Habibi lay down and refused to get up.

Ahmed pushed

and pulled

and pleaded, but Habibi would not budge.

"What's the matter, Habibi, my darling?" said Ahmed.
"Do you have a toothache?
Do you have a tummyache?"
Still, Habibi would not budge.

"Do your feet hurt?" asked Ahmed.
Habibi sighed a big sigh. Then he stood up.

"Here, darling," said Ahmed. "Take my babouches."

Habibi looked down at his slippered feet.
Then he ran off, slappity-slap, slappity-slap.
"Stop! Where are you going?" cried Ahmed,
running barefoot after him.

Habibi ran through the bazaar.

When he came to a shop where a man was selling
red fezzes with black tassels, he stopped.
Habibi nudged a fez with his nose.
"So you want a fez, do you?" said the shopkeeper,
and found one that fit Habibi perfectly.
"I'll trade you the hat for your babouches."
Habibi left the babouches and ran off,
ploppity-plop, ploppity-plop.

Ahmed finally reached the fez shop,
huffing and puffing, and had to bargain
for his very own babouches.

Habibi trotted through the bazaar, the black
tassel jouncing merrily atop his fez.
"What a handsome camel!"
he overheard people say as he
passed the gleaming brass
and tin shop.

"What an elegant camel!" people said as he passed the fruit and poultry markets.

Habibi held his head high as he pranced out of the bazaar.

Ahmed left the bazaar too, but he walked slowly and sadly.
He couldn't find his darling Habibi anywhere.

As he neared the camel ride stand, Ahmed's heart lept for joy. There was Habibi surrounded by happy, laughing children. He threw his arms around Habibi's neck.

"So that's what you wanted, my darling."

Then he stepped back to admire the fez.

"You are, indeed, the handsomest camel in all the land!"

Habibi gave every child an extra long ride.

At the end of the day, Habibi knelt down to let Ahmed climb aboard for the ride home.

"Thank you, my darling," said Ahmed.

"My feet are very sore from running after you all day."